LIZZIE McGUIRE MYSTERIES

HANDS OFF MY CRUSH-BOY!

By Lisa Banim
Based on the series
created by Terri Minsky

Watch it on
DISNEY CHANNEL
abc kids

DISNEY PRESS

VOLO

New York

Printed in the United States of America

First Edition
1 3 5 7 9 10 8 6 4 2

Library of Congress Catalog Card Number: 2003112345

ISBN 0-7868-4636-4
For more Disney Press fun, visit www.disneybooks.com
Visit DisneyChannel.com

CHAPTER 1

"Give that to me, you spiky-headed excuse for a brother!" Lizzie McGuire cried.

Matt McGuire held the glossy teen magazine behind his back. "Now, is that the way we ask nicely?" he said. "I don't think so."

"That's *my* brand-new issue of *Fave*," said Lizzie.

"Not anymore," Matt said. He ran down the hall to his room and locked himself inside.

"Mom!" Lizzie yelled.

"Let me handle this," said Miranda Sanchez.

Lizzie's best friend walked calmly to Matt's door and knocked. "Hey, Matt," she said sweetly. "Your little girlfriend Melina is downstairs. I'm sure she'll be very interested to hear you're a huge *Fave* fan. Makeup, fashion, boy bands . . ."

Matt's door opened. "Okay," he said, thrusting the magazine into Miranda's hands. "You guys can have it first. But there's a very important article in there that Lanny and I need to read."

"Like, what?" asked Lizzie, still fuming. "'Countdown to the Prom'?"

Matt sighed as he headed toward the stairs. "You wouldn't understand. It's business."

There should be some kind of contest for World's Most Annoying Little Brother. Then maybe i could actually *win* something for a change.

The girls hurried into Lizzie's bedroom. Miranda flopped on the bed and opened the magazine. "Lizzie, check this guy out," she said, holding up a big, glossy spread. "Is he adorable or what?"

"Definitely," Lizzie agreed, sitting next to Miranda.

The boy in the picture was gorgeous, all right. He had wavy blond hair and piercing blue eyes. And he was smiling as if he knew exactly how cute he was.

Miranda pointed to the headline of the article and read it. *Do you know a guy hotter than this one?*

Lizzie and Miranda looked at each other. "Yes!" they both answered at once.

"Ethan Craft is sooo much hotter," Lizzie said.

"How did I know you were going to say that?" Miranda teased. "But I have to agree."

Ethan was the cutest guy at Hillridge Junior High, and Lizzie had been crushing on him since forever. Unfortunately, Ethan hadn't yet realized that Lizzie was the perfect girlfriend for him—but that was only a matter of time as far as Lizzie was concerned.

"This guy's name is Ryan Rondale," Miranda said, still reading. "He's *Fave*'s reigning 'Mr. Teen Hottie.'"

"Hmm," Lizzie said, looking over Miranda's shoulder. "It says that any *Fave* reader can nominate their favorite hottie to compete against Ryan for this year's crown."

Miranda nodded. "All you have to do is e-mail the guy's photo and provide a personality profile. Easy," she said.

Lizzie flopped onto her back. "We *have* to nominate Ethan," she said, staring at the ceiling.

"Right," Miranda agreed. "We'd better ask him soon, though. The contest is only a month away."

Lizzie sat back up again. "*Ask* him?" she said. "No way. That would be totally embarrassing."

"Well, he's going to find out we nominated

him when the *Fave* people contact him," Miranda said. "We might as well be upfront about it."

Lizzie sighed. "Okay. So do *you* want to ask him?" she asked hopefully.

"Nope," Miranda said, shaking her head. "You're the one with the mongo crush. But no worries. Ethan will be totally flattered."

"I don't think I have the guts to ask him," Lizzie said. "Not in person, anyway."

Miranda shrugged. "Call him on the phone, then."

> Hello, Operator? Connect me to Hottie Central, please. i'd like to speak with Ethan Craft. My *name*? it's, uh . . . Ms. Lizzie i-Cannot-Possibly-Do-This!!!

Lizzie hugged a furry green pillow. "I don't

know," she said. "Maybe nominating Ethan isn't such a good idea. He'll think I'm really crushin' on him."

Miranda threw up her hands. "The whole world knows that, Lizzie. Why shouldn't he?"

Lizzie squeezed her eyes shut and reached for the phone next to her bed. "Here goes," she said as she dialed Ethan's number. She knew it by heart. Once she'd spent an entire Saturday afternoon deciding *not* to call him.

The phone rang on the other end of the line, and Ethan's stepmom answered. "Hold on, I'll get him," she told Lizzie.

"Hey, dude," Ethan said a minute later.

"Um, hi, Ethan, this is Lizzie," she said. "Lizzie McGuire."

"Well, yeah," Ethan said. "I only know one Lizzie, Lizzie. And that's you."

"Right," Lizzie said, twisting some hair around her finger. "Listen, I wanted to ask you something. . . ."

"Whoa," Ethan broke in. "That's awesome. I wanted to ask *you* something, too."

"Really?" Lizzie asked hopefully.

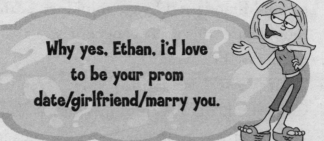

Why yes, Ethan, i'd love to be your prom date/girlfriend/marry you.

"Yeah," Ethan said. "Guess I was catching a few zzzs in Spanish class today. Do we have any homework?"

"No," Lizzie said, with a disappointed sigh. "We don't."

He likes me. He does. He's just a little too focused on appreciating me for my mind.

Miranda waved her arms to get Lizzie's attention. She made a speed-it-up-already gesture.

"I was th-thinking . . ." Lizzie stammered. "I mean, Miranda and I were thinking . . . that you should enter this really cool contest."

"Huh?" Ethan said.

"It's *Fave* Magazine's Mr. Teen Hottie Contest," Lizzie told him in a rush. "You know *Fave* magazine? Everyone at school reads it—"

Maybe if i talk *really* fast, it'll sound better.

"All you have to do is enter this pageant deal, you know?" Lizzie went on. "Really cool and really easy, and it's sponsored by U-Can Tan. You know, that instant tanning stuff?"

There was silence on the other end of the phone. *Uh-oh*, Lizzie thought.

"So if you win you get a scholarship, sports equipment, and a trip to Hawaii," she finished.

"And cold, hard cash!" Miranda called loudly from across the room.

Lizzie frowned at her friend. "So what do you think?" she asked Ethan.

"Did you say *Hawaii*, dude?" Ethan asked. "'Cause that'd be pretty cool."

"Right," Lizzie said eagerly. "You can surf there and everything. With the new board you'd win."

"New board, too? Hey, I really need a new board. What do I have to do again?" Ethan asked.

"Oh, not much," Lizzie assured him. "You just enter this contest. The only thing is, you have to be nominated first. And Miranda and I can do that."

"Awesome," Ethan said. "Okay, sign me up."

"Really?" Lizzie squealed. She gave Miranda a thumbs-up. "Great, Ethan. See you tomorrow at school. Bye."

"He said *yes*!" Lizzie cried, after hanging up. She danced around the room. "*Aloha*, Mr. Teen Hottie!"

Lizzie looked over the Mr. Teen Hottie application form. "Name, address, e-mail," she read. "Likes, Dislikes, Favorite Color, Favorite Group, Favorite Car, Favorite Food. And . . . an *essay*."

"An essay?" Miranda asked. "Does Ethan have to write it?"

Lizzie shook her head. "It doesn't say that exactly. We can handle it. You know, to save Ethan the hassle," she said. Then she found her Hillridge Junior High Yearbook. "And we've got the totally perfect Ethan photo to scan."

Ryan Rondale, you are so five minutes ago! My crush-boy's gonna crush you in the Mr. Teen Hottie competition!

"Can someone please tell me what's going on with Ethan Craft?" Gordo asked the next day at school. He was Lizzie and Miranda's other best friend.

"What do you mean, Gordo?" Lizzie asked.

"You mean, why is Ethan surrounded by even more girls than usual today?" Miranda asked.

"Well, they're blocking the halls," Gordo complained. "I was almost late for math class."

Just then, a tall blond cheerleader came barreling through the crowd. "Make way, people," Kate Sanders said. "I'm in a hurry here."

Lizzie cringed. She and Kate had actually been friends back in grade school. That was before Kate had turned majorly popular. And majorly snobby.

"I said, move it!" Kate screeched. "Hello? Ethan is waiting for me."

"You and fifty other fans," Gordo muttered.

Kate stopped in the middle of the hall and put her hands on her hips. "Excuse me? I happen to be Ethan's date for *Fave's* Mr. Teen Hottie pageant next month."

Lizzie's mouth dropped open. "How did you know about that?" she said.

"You mean Ethan asked *you*?" Miranda said.

"I repeat, will someone please tell me what's going on?" Gordo asked.

Kate rolled her eyes. "I *so* don't have time for this," she said. "But if you must know, *I* nominated Ethan for the Mr. Teen Hottie crown. So of course he's going to ask me to be his date."

"Wait a sec," Lizzie said. "Miranda and I nominated Ethan!"

"You did?" Gordo said. "That is so . . . lame." He jerked his head toward the end of the hall. "And it looks like you weren't the only ones."

Lizzie, Kate, and Miranda spun around. A smiling Ethan was now being swarmed by even more groupies.

"I c-can't b-believe it!" Lizzie sputtered. "Every girl at Hillridge must have sent in Ethan's name!"

"Well, we'll just see about that," Kate said, marching down the hall.

Gordo plucked Lizzie's copy of *Fave* from her

backpack. "Mind if I take a look at this Hottie pageant deal?" he asked.

Lizzie felt her face flame. "Um, sure, go ahead," she told him.

"Lizzie," Miranda said, "who's that dark-haired girl Kate is dissing right now? I've never seen her before."

Gordo glanced up from the magazine. "Oh, that's Madison Schwartz. She just moved here from New Jersey. She's my new science club partner. Sort of cute, huh?"

Lizzie crossed her arms. "I guess so," she said. But she was still thinking about Ethan.

i wanted to be Ethan's date for the contest. And now *i'm* going to be the one competing.

"Whoa, give me a break," Gordo said suddenly.

"This contest ad says Mr. Teen Hottie is a 'prestigious talent and scholarship competition.'"

"Yeah," Miranda said. "Your point?"

Gordo shook his head. "We're talking about Ethan Craft here. I mean, talent? Scholarship? Ethan?"

> Okay, maybe Gordo does have a point. Ethan isn't exactly a brainiac. And maybe his talents are a little . . . vague. But he's sweet and nice and cute. Did I mention cute?

"Gee, Gordo," Lizzie said. "We could nominate *you* for the contest, too." She glanced at Miranda. "We just didn't think you'd want us to."

"Right," Miranda said quickly. "We figured you wouldn't want to be up there on stage trying to show-off and stuff."

"Well . . . you're right. I mean, that's not my style at all," Gordo said.

"Of course not, Gordo," Lizzie said. She linked her arm through his and steered him down the hall.

Miranda took Gordo's other arm. "Yeah. And you wouldn't want every girl at Hillridge falling all over you like Ethan? That's not your style either, right?"

Gordo muttered something, but Lizzie wasn't listening. She couldn't stop thinking about Ethan and the contest. Ethan would need a lot of help to win the Mr. Teen Hottie title. And she, Lizzie McGuire, was a totally helpful person.

How could Ethan lose?

When Lizzie got home from school, she heard loud, terrible music blasting from the living room.

Toad Boy, Lizzie told herself, opening the front door.

Sure enough, her little brother and his friend Lanny were busting moves in front of the stereo. Matt's bossy little blond friend, Melina, was sitting on the couch, looking annoyed as usual. She had her own issue of *Fave* on her lap.

"No, no, no!" Melina called to the boys. "That was pathetic! Cut!"

Matt twirled around and hit the OFF button. "What's wrong, my sweet? That was perfect!"

"You call that perfect?" Melina crossed her arms. "Puh-leez. Again!"

"No, wait!" Lizzie cried, running toward the volume control. "What do you guys think you're doing?"

"You sound like Mom," Matt said. "By the way, she said to tell you she borrowed your earplugs. I think she's in the basement."

"Do you mind?" Melina asked Lizzie. "There's a rehearsal in progress here."

Lanny nodded in agreement. He never said very much. Actually, Lizzie had never heard him say anything at all.

"Congratulations, lucky sister," Matt said to Lizzie. "You are the first to witness the

L&M Experience. Well, after Mom, anyway."

"The *what*?" Lizzie said.

Matt pointed at Lanny and explained, "L is for Lanny." Then his arms made a jerky robot motion. "And M is for Matt. We're the next boy-band sensation."

"*If* I decide to become their manager," Melina said. She flipped past the boy band article in *Fave* to check out the new nail polish shades. "I have very high standards."

"Right," Lizzie said, heading upstairs. "Buh-bye."

"Hey, don't you want to stay and watch?" Matt called.

"No thanks," Lizzie said.

i'm betting math homework will be a lot less painful.

"So when do you think Ethan's going to hear about the contest?" Lizzie asked Miranda and Gordo at lunch the following week. "It's taking forever."

"Yeah, I'm surprised they didn't call him right away," Miranda said, dunking a French fry in barbecue sauce.

"Well, whenever they're ready, I'm ready," Gordo said. He patted his video camera beside him on the picnic bench. "I'm planning to shoot a behind-the-scenes-documentary of the Mr. Teen Hottie contest."

"That's a great idea, Gordo," Lizzie said.

Gordo shrugged. "I figure I need a little comedy for my video-clip portfolio."

Just then, a tall, blond woman in leopard-print spandex jeans and a bright purple top hurried into the school courtyard. Right behind her was a younger woman with short dark hair. She wore a black leather miniskirt, high-heeled boots, and a leather jacket.

"That's Ethan's stepmom!" Lizzie said.

"Yoo-hoo, Ethan!" Leopard Woman called. "Where are you, sweetie?"

The girls surrounding the table next to Lizzie and her friends stepped aside to let the two women through.

"Whoa," Miranda said. "Is that new girl Madison *feeding* Ethan his French fries?"

"I have the most fabulous news for you, honey," Mrs. Craft gushed to Ethan. "*Fave* Magazine just called. You're in the contest!"

Ethan opened his mouth for another fry. "Cool," he said.

"And I have even more fantastic news," his stepmom added. "My cousin here, Amanda Littlefield, is a professional publicist and manager. She's going to coach you through the *Fave* contest. Isn't that terrific, darling?"

"I can't believe this," Lizzie whispered to Miranda and Gordo. "Ethan doesn't need any more help. I mean, he's going to have *me*."

"Sorry, Lizzie. Amanda Littlefield is famous," Gordo said. "I've seen her interviewed on the *Music 24/7* channel. She's managed some pretty successful boy bands over the past few years. And besides, she looks like a total rocker babe."

Lizzie just glared at him.

Amanda stepped toward Ethan, practically knocking over Madison, Kate, and the plate of fries. "It's wonderful to finally meet you in person, Ethan. Your stepmom has told me sooo much about you. And since I'm, er, free of responsibilities at the moment, I can be your official pageant coach."

"That woman is so fake," said Miranda.

"Well, I think it's disgusting the way everyone's overwhelming Ethan," Lizzie said. "Maybe, if I play it cool, he'll notice I really like him for who he is. Not just the future Mr. Teen Hottie."

"Sure, Lizzie," said Miranda, glancing back at the crowd of females around Ethan. "Good luck with that."

CHAPTER

3

"**T**his is so incredibly awesome," Miranda told Lizzie a few weeks later. "We're at the opening dinner for the Mr. Teen Hottie Contest—and totally surrounded by . . . hotties!" She smiled at the cute guy sitting at the table next to them in the huge banquet hall. He had short, dark hair and amazing blue eyes.

"At least we're sitting at Ethan's table," Lizzie said. "Even if some of the other girls who nominated him get to sit here, too."

"When do we eat?" Ethan said, eyeing the bread basket. "I'm getting kinda hungry."

Beside him, Amanda Littlefield put her hand over his. "Just hold on," she said, smiling toward the podium at the front of the room. "Manners make a good first impression."

Amanda was wearing a short, gold sequined dress and pointy gold shoes. Lizzie had changed her own outfit five times before she'd decided on a hot-pink sparkle top and black leather skirt. At least Lizzie could give herself snaps for coolness. Kate Sanders's little black designer dress and string of pearls may have been way expensive, but to Lizzie they seemed way boring.

"Shh!" Kate told Amanda sharply. Then she caught herself. "I mean, look, everyone, there's the master of ceremonies. Ty Wiley!"

A handsome older man in a tuxedo walked up to the podium. Lizzie could see Gordo filming from behind a curtain.

"Good evening, everyone," Ty said into the

microphone. "And welcome to this year's Mr. Teen Hottie Contest, sponsored by every teen girl's fave magazine: *Fave* Magazine!" He chuckled at his own joke. Everyone clapped politely.

"Oh boy," Miranda said. "Does this guy do game shows too?"

"Soap operas," Kate snapped. "Where have *you* been living, under a rock?"

Ty invited each of the five hottie contestants to come up, introduce himself, and serenade the audience with a karaoke song of his choice.

Karaoke? Can Ethan *sing*? Oh, no. i don't think i can watch this. Not to mention listen.

Each of the guys took a turn singing. Finally, it was Ethan's turn. Lizzie held her breath when he started his song.

The other guys had picked slow love ballads, but Ethan chose a popular rap song. A minute into it, everyone was clapping to the beat. Ethan was a hit!

"I guess it doesn't actually matter that he isn't the greatest singer," Lizzie told Miranda.

Miranda nodded. "Yeah, there's just something about Ethan that everybody likes."

"He's really enthusiastic. And he can energize a crowd," said Lizzie.

"The boy's got star quality," Amanda observed, watching him bounce down off the stage and into the audience. "I know how to spot it."

After the contestants returned to their tables, dinner was served. Ethan was just stuffing a forkload of lasagna into his mouth when Ryan Rondale, the current Mr. Teen Hottie, appeared.

"So you're Ethan Craft," he said, holding out his hand. "I'm Ryan Rondale. But I guess you knew that already."

Ryan smiled big. To Lizzie, it didn't seem

genuine. "There's something about Ryan I don't like," she whispered to Miranda. "I don't think he's happy that everyone liked Ethan's song."

"It's those eyes," Miranda said. "They kind of look right through you." She turned around and smiled again at the dark-haired hottie at the next table. "That guy Grant Castle has *nice* eyes."

"I just wanted to wish you luck," Ryan said to Ethan.

Ethan swallowed another hunk of lasagna. "Thanks, dude. You too."

"Right. May the best man win," Ryan said. He started to go, then suddenly turned to Kate. "Excuse me," he said. "Have we met?"

"No," Kate said. Then she smiled.

Ryan flashed another fake grin. "I could never forget meeting a girl as pretty as you. There's an empty place at my table. Care to join me?"

Lizzie almost choked on her ice water.

Kate stood up quickly. "Sure, Ryan," she said. "I'll see you later, Ethan, okay?"

"Gee, leaving so soon?" Miranda said.

Kate threw her and Lizzie a withering glance as she swept past. "This table's a little crowded," she told Ryan sweetly. "With losers," she hissed over her shoulder—just loud enough for Lizzie and Miranda to hear.

"Oooh, that cheer-witch makes me so mad," Miranda said through gritted teeth.

"At least she didn't bring her pom-pom posse with her this time," Lizzie said. She frowned. "But don't you think it's sort of strange that Ryan invited Kate to his table, just like that?"

"I can't believe she dumped Ethan, just like that," Miranda said.

Lizzie looked across the table. Her hottie crush-boy seemed okay with that. He was talking to Madison and Amanda. Well, actually, they were the ones doing the talking. And it looked more like fawning—all over him.

"Here's my guess," said Lizzie. "Ryan probably knows Ethan's going to be his biggest competition. So he's going to use Kate to find out more about Ethan."

"Maybe," said Miranda. She glanced at the dark-haired boy at the next table. "But Ethan's not the only threat to Ryan. I think Grant Castle is pretty hot, too."

Just then, the contest host, Ty Wiley, tapped on the microphone. "Contestants and guests, your attention, please," he said. "It's time to explain how our contest works."

The host went on to describe the Teen Hottie events. "Tomorrow morning, our five contestants will ride in the Parade of Floats down Main Street. They'll be judged on presentation."

"Parade?" Ethan said blankly.

"No problem, sugar," Amanda told him. "You don't have to do a thing. Just wave."

"Next," continued Ty, "we'll all get to know our contestants through the Q&A event, which is an intensive question-and-answer panel. And tomorrow night's Rate-a-Date event will ask contestants to respond to dating questions posed from select girls in the audience."

"Now *that's* more like it," Miranda said.

"The second day of our pageant starts with the always entertaining Dancing Dudes event," Ty announced. "That's when our own special dudes will be judged on their moves."

"Cool," Ethan said. "I've got awesome moves."

Lizzie glanced worriedly at Miranda. They both remembered the last time they'd seen Ethan "dance." It was entertaining, all right. But not in a good way.

"Leave the choreography to me," Amanda told Ethan. "I'm a pro, remember?"

"And the final evening's events will include the talent competition, followed by a walk down the aisle in prom wear with a girl of each contestant's choice, and a very important final question."

Lizzie glanced at Ethan. He looked as if he'd gone into shock. "Whoa," he said. "That sounds like a lot of pressure. And I'm not real good at pressurized stuff."

At last, a chance for me to show Ethan what a great, supportive, wonderful friend I can be—and *friend* is halfway to *girlfriend*, oh yeah!

"Don't worry, Ethan," Lizzie said quickly. "You'll do fine. Really. I believe in you, and I'm right here to help."

"Me too," Madison added, just as quickly.

"Ethan, babe, you just have a teeny bit of stage fright," Amanda said with a wave of her hand. "It happens to my clients all the time. Trust me."

Lizzie nudged Miranda and rolled her eyes.

"Well, she's the expert," whispered Miranda.

"But *she* didn't nominate Ethan. *We* did," Lizzie pointed out.

"Now, Ethan," Amanda continued, "I'm not

too happy about the fine print on this contract you signed. The Teen Hottie winner is obligated to a one-year commitment to publicize U-Can Tan. Why didn't you show this to me first?"

"The U-Can Tan dude told me just to sign it," Ethan said. "Sorry."

"No problem," Amanda said. "That's why I'm here. To look out for you."

Five minutes later, a DJ started spinning tunes. Everybody got up to dance.

"Ethan looks totally psyched again," Lizzie told Miranda as they stepped on the dance floor.

"Yeah," Miranda said, though her eyes were on Grant Castle. "Let's just hope his 'awesome' dance moves don't injure anybody."

For the next hour, Lizzie danced with Ethan, Miranda, and Madison—who fortunately made a lot of trips to the ladies room. Kate, of course, was dancing with Ryan Rondale.

Amanda started to dance, too, until she got a cell phone call and ducked out to the lobby.

Finally, the music stopped. The Mr. Teen Hottie opening reception was officially over.

"Well, that was cool," Lizzie said, as everyone returned to their tables to get their things.

"Yeah," Miranda said. "I even got to dance with Grant. He's soooo cute!"

"Miranda!" Lizzie said. "You're as bad as Kate. We have to stay focused on *Ethan*, remember?"

Just then, they heard Ethan say, "Whoa, dudes! What's this?"

Lizzie whirled around. Ethan was staring at his party-favor bottle of U-Can Tan sunblock.

He held it out to Lizzie, frowning. "Check it out," he said.

Lizzie took the bottle and gasped. Someone had written in big black letters on the label:

DON'T GET BURNED. DROP OUT NOW!

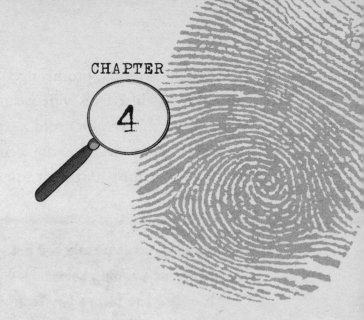

"Ohmigosh, Ethan, this is *terrible*!" cried Lizzie.

"Yeah," Ethan said. "It says here U-Can Tan goes on invisible, then turns your skin tan in half an hour. That is really weird, dude."

Miranda rolled her eyes. "No, Ethan. Not *that* part of the label. Those are the directions. Lizzie's talking about the words written in black marker."

Just then, Gordo spoke up. He had finished his filming and was hanging out at their table.

"You know, that 'drop-out-now' part of the

warning actually sounds promising." With a little smile, Gordo lifted his video camera and pointed it at Ethan. "I've never sold *news* footage before. Maybe Ethan will be the center of a global conspiracy against hotties or something."

Obviously, *some* people are not taking this warning seriously. A threat to the future Mr. Teen Hottie is a threat to . . . to . . . world peace!

"Don't worry, Ethan," Lizzie said. "I can find out who's trying to make you drop out of the contest. I'm pretty good at solving mysteries."

"Drop out of the contest?" Ethan looked confused. "Whoa, dude, I'm not dropping out. I'm going to Hawaii!"

"Ethan, someone just sent you a threat," Lizzie pointed out patiently.

Ethan laughed. "Lizzie, Lizzie, Lizzie. It's just some kind of joke."

"Sorry, but I don't think so," Lizzie said. "You could be in real danger."

"Look, Lizzie, I appreciate the offer," Ethan said. "But really, everything is cool."

Just then, Madison came pushing through the departing crowd. "Ethan!" she called. "I've got your Mr. Teen Hottie sweatshirt!"

"Guess I better go," Ethan said, as Madison bounded up. "But, hey, why don't all you guys come to the parade tomorrow? You can ride on my float."

"We'd love to," Lizzie said quickly. Miranda nodded.

"Me, too," Madison chimed in. She held up a hot pink Mr. Teen Hottie sweatshirt and a larger blue one. "Aren't these cute, Ethan? Now we can match."

Gordo clapped Ethan on the shoulder. "Better count me off the float. My job is to capture every thrilling moment for posterity." He held up his camera. "But you have fun. Okay?"

"Sure, dude," said Ethan. "Whatever."

"Well, I guess Ethan isn't too worried about that warning," Miranda said to Lizzie as they left the banquet hall with Gordo.

Ethan was in front of them, heading out the door with a bunch of admiring fans from the reception. Madison was attached to his arm like a barnacle.

"I guess not," Lizzie said with a sigh. "But I'm going to be on the lookout anyway."

"Well, it'll be tough," Miranda said. "The culprit could have been practically anyone in the room tonight." She smiled over her shoulder at Grant Castle, who smiled back. "*Almost* anyone."

"Yeah," Lizzie said. "But *remember*, the people with the biggest motive are Ethan's hottie rivals. They *all* want to win the contest."

"Well, I'd keep my eye on that guy," Gordo said, nodding toward Ryan Rondale. Ryan was greeting fans and signing autographs as they passed.

"Definitely," Lizzie agreed. "But let's not count out that two-faced Kate."

"Yeah," Miranda said. "Looks like she's doing the meet-and-greet over there, too. Who would want Ryan's *date's* autograph? Puh-leez."

"Mmmmm," Lizzie said. But she couldn't help imagining herself by Ethan's side, dressed in a pink prom dress, complete with diamond tiara.

It's a tough job keeping the world safe for the future Mr. Teen Hottie. Yeah. Hard work, sacrifice, plus killer shoes and a lot of lip gloss!

* * *

"Will you stop squishing me?" Lizzie told Matt in the back seat of the car the next morning. Mrs. McGuire was dropping them and Miranda downtown for the big Mr. Teen Hottie Parade. Gordo had left earlier to get some footage of Ethan getting ready.

"I can't help it," Matt said. "I need more room than you do. I have to stay stretched out and loose for my networking thing."

"*Networking* thing?" Lizzie said.

"Yes," said Matt. "I'm setting up an audition."

"For what?" asked Lizzie. "Mr. Preteen Hot *Not-tie*?"

"For your information," snapped Matt, "Lanny and I are taking the L&M Experience to the next level. We'll be on the lookout for agents and talent scouts among the contest attendees. That's what's called *networking*, sister dear."

Lizzie groaned.

He is *so* not my brother. My parents found him under a toadstool.

Miranda turned around in the front seat. "Sweet outfit there, Matt," she said. "That banana yellow jumpsuit with the fringe is very . . . Las Vegas."

The girls and Matt jumped out of the car as soon as Mrs. McGuire pulled up at the convention center. "I'll pick you up at the other end of the parade route, okay? And be sure to watch out for your brother now, Lizzie!" Mrs. McGuire called loudly from the car window.

Lizzie squeezed her eyes shut. How totally embarrassing.

How can Mom expect me to babysit that annoying little twerp? i have some serious detective work to do here!

But when she opened her eyes again, Matt had already vanished into the crowd. Zillions of people were waiting for the parade to start.

"Don't worry," Miranda said. "With that Big Bird-meets-Elvis number he's wearing, he'll be easy to find."

"Lizzie, Miranda! Yoo-hoo!" someone called.

The girls turned to see Madison hurrying toward them. She was wearing a tropical-print halter top and a short grass skirt.

"You're going to have to change fast, guys," Madison said. "The parade is about to start."

"Huh?" Lizzie and Miranda said together.

Madison grabbed them both and steered them toward a side entrance to the convention center. "The costume room is down the hall on the left," she said. "You need to be in full Hawaiian gear."

"No way," Miranda said flatly.

Madison frowned. "It's for *Ethan*," she said. "Everyone riding on the floats has to be in costume."

Lizzie sighed. She didn't want to ride down Main Street as a hula girl. On the other hand, she had to stay close to Ethan. *Very* close.

"So tell me everything you know about Ethan," Madison said to Lizzie and Miranda as they entered the costume room.

Hmmmm, Lizzie thought. There's something about Madison I don't trust. She just moved here from another state—yet she's totally head over heels for Ethan already. Is it really a mongo crush? Or is there something else going on? Last night, she kept leaving the dance floor. Had she really gone to the restroom all those times? Or was *she* the one who'd written that warning on the U-Can Tan bottle? But why would she want to sabotage Ethan?

"I need all kinds of details," Madison gushed on. "I mean, it looks like neither of you is Ethan's girlfriend or anything. So he's up for grabs, right?"

Lizzie's mouth dropped open. So did Miranda's.

> **For the record, i am GOING to be Ethan's girlfriend. So hands off!**

Lizzie was about to reply to Madison when she heard a voice coming from behind a nearby garment rack.

"Hey, babe, I can't really talk now," Amanda Littlefield was saying into her cell phone. "I have to go to this stupid parade. I would have called you earlier, but I got stuck talking to these two annoying little wanna-be boy band brats."

Lizzie gritted her teeth. She had to be talking about Matt and Lanny.

"They asked me about 'connections' in the music biz," Amanda went on. "Can you believe the *nerve*? Anyway, I just had to tell you . . ."

Amanda's voice dropped. Lizzie took a few steps closer to the garment rack. "Stall!" she silently mouthed to Miranda.

"Sooo, um, Madison," Miranda said, steering the dark-haired girl toward the other side of the room. "Where can I find a cute grass skirt *exactly* like yours?"

Lizzie leaned so far back to eavesdrop that she nearly knocked over the garment rack.

"I have found a *very* interesting new prospect," Lizzie heard Amanda say. "If I play my cards right, this could be the big break I've been needing so badly. You know, after my career hit that little . . . slump?"

Lizzie gasped and quickly covered her mouth.

But it was too late. Amanda had heard her! "Gotta go, babe," she said abruptly. "We'll talk later." She snapped her cell phone shut and click-click-clicked out of the costume room in her black spike heels.

Hmmmm, Lizzie thought. Was Amanda talking about Ethan. And if she was, what was he an "interesting new prospect" for?

"Lizzie, Lizzie, Lizzie!" Ethan called, pounding on the costume room door. "Where are you?"

Lizzie burst out into the hall. "Is everything okay? Did you get another threat?"

Ethan shook his head. "Negative-o. Gordo sent me to get you 'cause the parade's about to start." He raised one eyebrow. "Is that your costume?"

Lizzie looked down at her flowered pink capris and tank top. "Um, yeah," she said. "It is now."

"Cool," Ethan said. He was wearing a Hawaiian shirt, shades, surfer jams, and flip-flops.

Outside, Lizzie and Ethan climbed onto the float. Amanda, Madison, Miranda, and a bunch of other Hillridge girls in hula costumes were already there.

"Can you believe these floats?" Miranda told Lizzie. "They are so incredibly tacky."

Lizzie frowned. Miranda was right. The U-Can Tan trailers had been covered with fake flowers, seashells, and U-Can Tan ads. Speakers on the floats were playing lame luau music.

"Hey guys, give me a nice big wave," Gordo called to Lizzie and Miranda from the sidewalk. He was laughing so hard he could hardly hold his camera straight. "Say pineapple!"

Lizzie and Miranda both glared at him.

"Okay, everybody, let's get this show on the road," Ty Wiley boomed into a megaphone from the lead float. "Gentlemen, start your floats!"

"How do these things work?" Ethan asked.

Amanda patted his arm. "You don't have to do anything," she assured him. "It's taken care of."

Each of the trailers was hooked up to an SUV. Their vehicle started up and the trailer lurched. Lizzie and Miranda grabbed each other for balance as the float rolled down the street.

"Yes indeed, folks, everybody loves a parade!" Ty Wiley's voice blared through the megaphone. "And everybody loves U-Can Tan products—and this year's hot Mr. Teen Hottie contestants!"

All the contestants waved from their floats as Ty introduced them. Ryan Rondale, who was riding on the float ahead of them, flashed his plastic smile. Beside him, Kate blew fake-o kisses to the crowd.

"Oh, puh-leeeze," Miranda said. "She makes me want to hurl."

Lizzie struggled to keep her balance on the jerking float. "Don't say that, okay?" she pleaded. "This float is making me kind of queasy."

Behind them, Grant Castle was riding with his black lab, Rudi, and a group of surfer girls.

"Doesn't he look cute?" Miranda said, sighing. "I hope those girls are just his cousins or something."

"Miranda, get a grip," Lizzie said. She noted that Amanda and Madison were standing close to Ethan, fawning all over him. It made her feel even more queasy.

Lizzie felt the float give another huge lurch. "Ohmigosh!" she cried. "It's breaking!"

"What?" Miranda said. Her eyes widened as the float detached from its SUV and headed down the hill. As the float gathered speed, it began to swerve toward the curb. People along the sidewalk lunged out of the way.

"Yikes, we're going to crash!" Miranda shouted.

"Cool!" Ethan exclaimed. "This is totally awesome, dudes!"

The float bounced off a curb, and came to a stop in the middle of the street—backward.

Attention, this is your detective speaking. We hope you enjoyed your ride with us today. Please keep your seat belts fastened and yourselves in the upright position. Buh-bye!

"First the sunblock warning, now this," Lizzie told Miranda. "Someone really *is* trying to scare Ethan out of the contest."

"Uh, he doesn't look too scared," Miranda said.

Lizzie glanced at Ethan and the crowd of hula girls. They were laughing hysterically. So were Ryan and Kate on the float ahead. Ryan gave everyone on Ethan's float a wave as his own float just kept moving down the road.

But two people were suddenly missing from Ethan's float, Lizzie noticed—Amanda and Madison!

Where did they go? Lizzie wondered. Immediately suspicious, she jumped to the ground—and ran straight into Grant Castle.

"Whoa!" she cried.

"Gee, I'm sorry," Grant said. "I saw what happened to your float. So I stopped to see if you were all okay."

"Yeah, I think so," said Lizzie. She glanced up at the float. Ethan and the girls were now having a fake-flower fight. Miranda smiled down at Grant, and Grant smiled back.

Was *Grant* the person who'd sabotaged Ethan's float? Lizzie wondered. Was he trying to be a big hero now—just *pretending* to be all worried?

And where the heck were Amanda and Madison?

Lizzie quickly spotted Amanda on the sidewalk. The manager was yelling loudly into her cell phone. "I'm telling you, we're not going to stand for this kind of treatment," she was saying. "My client is very upset. I'm going to pull him straight out of this contest, you worm!"

Oooo-kay, thought Lizzie, I guess the *whole world* knows where Amanda is now. But where's Madison?

Lizzie moved around the float—and found her at the front of it, kneeling on the ground near the trailer hitch. The girl was sticking something into the waistband of her fake grass skirt.

Aha! Lizzie thought. The pin for the trailer hitch!

"Hold it right there, Madison!" Lizzie called, running toward her. "Consider yourself *busted*!"

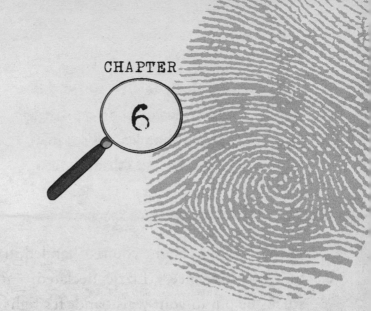

Madison stared at Lizzie with big, innocent brown eyes. "What do you mean, 'busted'? What did I do?"

Lizzie crossed her arms and frowned. "You were the one who loosened that hitch pin so Ethan's trailer would detach from the SUV."

Madison shook her head. "You're crazy. I'd never do anything like that. I *love* Ethan!" She blushed. "I mean, I really, really like him."

i really feel sorry for this girl. i mean, she's crushin' so hard she's lost all sense of reality. As Ethan's future wife, i can easily see that!

"Madison, I caught you red-handed, trying to hide the evidence," Lizzie declared. "You just stuck the pin in your waistband. It's right there."

Madison stood up and pulled the pin out of her skirt. "Oh, you mean this? That's right, Lizzie. It is the pin. But I *just* found it here on the ground."

Yeah, Lizzie thought, *sure* you did.

"It's true," Madison went on. "Right after the float crashed, I rushed over to see if I could find out why. And I did." She waved the pin in front of Lizzie's face. "You're just jealous, because *I* found it first."

"No way!" Lizzie cried. "I don't believe you."

"Too bad," Madison said. "Because I'm going to show this to Ethan right now." She ran back and climbed up onto the float, fluffing her hair as she rushed over to him.

"Yo, Ms. McGuire," called a boy's voice, "can you tell us exactly what happened to your float?"

Lizzie whirled around. Gordo had been standing there with his camera pointed at her.

"Not now, Gordo," Lizzie said, waving him away. "I have to think about this case."

"Can't you think while you're giving your best friend an exclusive interview?" Gordo asked.

"No," Lizzie said. Then she thought of something. "Hey, Gordo, did you get *everything* on tape? You may have caught the person who sabotaged Ethan's float!"

"Sorry, Lizzie," Gordo said. "I was filming those surfer girls on Grant's float."

"Aaargh!" Lizzie cried in frustration.

"You know, that pin could have come loose by itself," Gordo noted. "It could have been an accident. Madison might have been telling the truth. I mean, why would she do it?"

"Maybe to come to Ethan's rescue," said Lizzie. "If Ethan's in trouble, she gets to save him. Get it."

Gordo nodded. "Yeah . . . I see where you're going—you think Madison's, like, a whack-job arsonist who *sets* the fire himself so he can be a big hero and call 9-1-1."

"Exactly," said Lizzie. Then she sighed. "Or not. I mean, I don't trust Madison, but I didn't actually *see* her do anything more than pick up the dropped hitch pin. The guilty party might still be another contestant."

"Tough case," said Gordo with a little smile.

Lizzie wasn't sure whether Gordo was amused or impressed. "Well," she said, "I might as well get back on the float. I should keep an even closer eye on Ethan now."

"I'll come with you," Gordo told her. "Not that I want to ride on that stupid thing," he added quickly. "I'll just be there to film every-thing, in case."

"Thanks, Gordo," Lizzie said.

As she and Gordo climbed on board, Miranda called out. "Hey, you guys, guess what? We're going to get to ride on Grant's float! Isn't that nice of him?"

"Um, yeah," Lizzie said. But she wasn't sure how nice a guy Grant really was. He was still one of Ethan's rivals.

"Grant told me that his little sister sent in his profile to *Fave*," Miranda gushed on. "He just entered the contest so he could get scholarship money to go to vet school someday. Isn't that cool?"

"Mmmmm," Lizzie said. A likely story, she told herself. Did Grant really want to help animals? Or was he in this contest to be famous and go to Hawaii?

Lizzie, Miranda, Gordo, Ethan, and his entire entourage piled onto Grant's float.

Through his megaphone, Ty Wiley announced what a nice guy Grant Castle was to make room on his own float for Ethan, and the whole crowd started chanting Grant's name. Grant was a hero—and the definite winner of the parade event.

Ryan Rondale strode up to Grant and Ethan's float. His own trailer had already reached the end of the parade, but no one had paid any attention.

Ryan reached up to shake hands with Grant and Ethan. "Congratulations," he said with a huge smile. Then Lizzie heard him add through his teeth, "Enjoy your fifteen seconds of fame, guys. It won't last."

Grant shrugged at Ryan and waved to the crowd.

"Thanks, dude," Ethan said to Ryan, thinking it was some kind of sage advice.

As soon as the float reached the end of the parade route, Ty Wiley rushed up to them and said, "All right, kids, this event's a wrap. Now it's time to prepare for this afternoon's next big event—the Q&A!"

"That's the question-and-answer panel," Amanda reminded Ethan in a low voice.

"So listen up, contestants," Ty went on. "You can all head back to the convention center right now to pick up your envelopes containing the questions for the Q&A portion of our contest. Each of you is strongly encouraged to review the questions and consider your answers before appearing on stage."

"In other words," Gordo whispered to Lizzie and Miranda, "we 'encourage' you to 'consider' answering with something other than 'Duh.'"

Lizzie and Miranda looked at each other in horror. "That's right," said Gordo. "Ethan's toast."

Lizzie had to admit that answering questions wasn't one of Ethan's strengths.

"Hey, I didn't know studying was going to be part of this deal," Ethan said. He looked worried.

"Forget preparing answers then, sugar,"

Amanda said, with a wave. "You're better off using the time to practice for the Dancing Dudes event tomorrow. I'd be happy to show you some moves. I do choreography for *all* my clients."

"No, wait!" Lizzie broke in. Amanda glared at her. "Miranda and Gordo and I can help you study, Ethan. And my mom will give us a ride back to the convention center."

"Yeah, sure, I'll go with you guys," said Ethan. "But we need to stop at the Burger Barn on the way. I can't think on an empty stomach."

"Or a full one, either," Lizzie heard Gordo mutter. She nudged him with her elbow.

"Well, fine," Amanda said, looking peeved. "You go right ahead then, Ethan. I'll just take my new red Ferrari."

"Can I come too, Ms. Littlefield?" Madison asked quickly. "I need to get to the convention center right away."

Hmmm, Lizzie thought. Why is she in such a big hurry?

"Sure, kid. Whatever," said Amanda, whipping her cell phone out of her purse. She began to punch in numbers. "Just don't talk to me on the way, okay? I have to concentrate on my driving."

"Well, let's go, Ethan," Lizzie said, taking him by the arm. "Don't worry, getting ready for the Q&A event is going to be totally fun."

"And totally useless," Gordo muttered.

Lizzie hoped Gordo was wrong. Still, helping Ethan come up with intelligent, event-winning answers wasn't going to be a cakewalk.

Can Ethan Craft be coached to look clever and quick-witted in under two hours? . . . Uh, i'll get back to you on that.

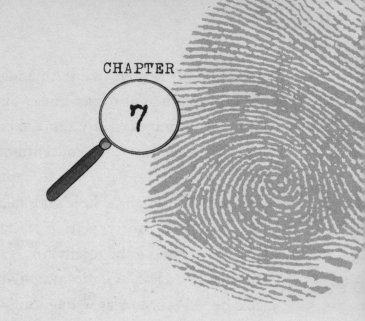

CHAPTER

7

"I am *so* stuffed!" Miranda moaned. "Why did you guys let me eat *two* Triple-Moo Burgers?"

"And fries, dude," Ethan said happily. "Udderly Large fries."

Gordo shook his head. "Gotta love the Burger Barn. 'Clog your arteries in three minutes or less—and that's our guarantee!'"

"We'd better pick up your envelope and get started on those questions, Ethan," Lizzie said. She looked around the lobby of the convention center. "There must be a Mr. Teen Hottie table set up somewhere."

Just then, Madison came running up to them. She was waving a large white envelope. "Ethan, I've got your questions! And I started writing down some answers for you, too!"

"Gee, thanks, Madison," Ethan said, taking the packet. "That was really nice of you."

"Well, actually, Amanda got there before me and picked it up," Madison admitted. "But she had to take a private phone call, so she gave it to me and told me to go find you."

"So, is there anything else you need, Ethan?" Madison asked. "How about a soda?"

"Thanks, that'd be cool," Ethan said. "Grape, okay?" Madison scurried off to find it.

Gordo tapped his watch and whispered to Lizzie and Miranda. "Hey guys, it's study time. We only have an hour left to prep Mr. Teen Brainiac here."

"Yikes," Lizzie said. "Let's go into that empty meeting room over there."

For the next forty-five minutes, Lizzie, Miranda, and Gordo tried to help Ethan remember answers. Even after Madison brought his grape soda to perk him up, it was a tough job.

"Unbelievable," Gordo said in disgust. "The questions are all about U-Can Tan products."

"I'll never remember this stuff," Ethan said.

"Don't get discouraged," Lizzie told him. "Why don't we try some memory hooks?"

Ethan stared at her. "Huh?" he said.

Lizzie had tutored Ethan in math once. It was possible that this would work. She thought fast. "Like here, question one. 'What is the best way to protect yourself from dangerous UV rays?' The answer is, *use U-Can Tan sunblock*, right?"

"I guess so," Ethan said.

"So you could turn it into a rap lyric," suggested Miranda. "'Question one is tons of fun, I use sunblock when I'm under the sun.' Get it?"

Ethan tried to spin his grape soda bottle. "Yeah. That's cool. How many questions are there?"

"Twenty." Lizzie sighed.

Twenty questions isn't funny,
when is this torture gonna
be done-ie?

Two more bottles of grape soda later, it was time for the Q&A event. Ethan seemed totally confident as he took his place on the stage with the four other contestants.

Lizzie and Miranda sat in Ethan's cheering section between Madison and Amanda.

This is good. i can keep an
eye on both suspects at
once. (One eye per suspect.)

Gordo was filming again—from the side of the stage. Lizzie had asked him to keep his camera on Ryan and Grant, just in case they tried any dirty tricks.

"All right, folks," Ty Wiley said from the podium. "It's time for our tough Q&A event. And question number one is for Mr. Hottie contestant—Ethan Craft!"

Lizzie held her breath. Would Ethan remember the right answers?

"Ethan, here we go: What is the effect of UV rays on the human body? You have exactly twenty seconds to answer."

Lizzie's eyes widened in horror. That wasn't question one! Not the one they'd prepped Ethan for, anyway. The question was supposed to be: "What is the best way to protect yourself from dangerous UV rays?"

What was going on? wondered Lizzie.

"Uh, w-well . . ." Ethan stammered, "UV rays go straight through your skeleton, dude. Like at the doctor."

Lizzie covered her eyes. "Ohmigosh," she

whispered to Miranda. "He's talking about X-rays!"

"The judges are gonna freak," Miranda said.

Then Ethan smiled as if he'd just remembered the memory hook. Quickly, he rapped, "And I use U-Can Tan sunblock when I'm under the sun."

Ty Wiley looked extremely pleased. He glanced to the side of the stage and asked, "Will our panel of judges accept that answer?"

One of the women at the judges' table looked at Ethan. Then she smiled and nodded.

All the girls in the crowd cheered.

"All right then, folks," Ty said. "On to question two. Ryan, what president said, 'Do what you can with what you have, where you are'?"

"That would be Teddy Roosevelt, Ty," Ryan answered smoothly.

Lizzie sunk all the way down in her seat. "None of the questions Ethan studied will work," she whispered to Miranda. "These are all different questions!"

"Do you think someone switched the questions in Ethan's envelope?" Miranda asked.

Lizzie looked over at Madison. The girl had had her hands on both that hitch pin at the parade *and* Ethan's envelope. And hadn't she said she'd started writing down the answers for him? Maybe she'd started writing *new questions,* too!

The Q&A session dragged on. Lizzie could hardly bear to listen. But somehow, Ethan managed to come off okay.

"In what state was famous hottie Elvis Presley's hit movie *Blue Hawaii* filmed?" asked Ty.

Ethan looked at the emcee blankly. "Sorry, Mr. Ty, dude, what was the question again? Something, um . . . Hawaii?"

Ty beamed as the buzzer sounded. "Cowabunga, Ethan! The answer is indeed *Hawaii*!"

Everyone in the audience clapped for Ethan.

"Awesome," Ethan said, shrugging.

"He's definitely lucking out," Miranda whispered to Lizzie.

"And this audience loves him," Lizzie said, looking around. "He's coming off as really easy-going and genuine."

Grant Castle seemed far too nervous up there in the hot seat. And Ryan, whose last question had been a tough one about Benjamin Franklin, was looking the most uncool of all. He kept fidgeting and fiddling with the cuff of his long-sleeved shirt.

He's losing his cool, Lizzie thought. But he's still getting all of his answers right. Strange.

As the curtain finally closed on the Q&A event, Ethan and Grant gave each other friendly high fives. The two of them—and Ryan Rondale—had come off the best out of the five.

"I'll meet you and Gordo backstage," Lizzie whispered to Miranda. "I'm going to follow Ryan. Keep an eye on Madison and Amanda, okay?"

"Sure," Miranda said, rolling her eyes. "That'll be so much fun."

Lizzie hurried to the stage door to wait for the contestants. She wasn't the only one who wanted to see the hotties. Girls with cameras and autograph books were everywhere.

Good, Lizzie told herself. She plastered herself against the wall as the guys came out. Ethan and Grant were immediately surrounded with fans, but Ryan pushed his admirers aside—even Kate.

"Sorry, gotta go," he told them, smiling apologetically. "Hottie duties, you know."

Lizzie's eyes narrowed. *Hottie duties?* Puhleeze, she thought as Ryan turned and walked quickly down the hall.

I have to follow him, Lizzie told herself. He could be planning the next way to sabotage Ethan—or someone else.

But as Ryan turned a corner, he started fiddling with his sleeve again.

Why doesn't he just roll them up? Lizzie wondered. Long, buttoned sleeves wasn't exactly a stylin' look.

Suddenly, Ryan pulled what looked like a small index card from his sleeve. He ripped it up and tossed the pieces into a nearby trash can.

As the reigning Mr. Teen Hottie headed into the guys' dressing room, Lizzie lunged at the trash. Quickly, she put together the pieces of the torn card.

"Do what you can with what you have," she read. "Teddy Roosevelt."

Ryan hadn't even bothered to memorize the answers, Lizzie realized. What a sneak!

She hurried to find Miranda and Gordo. But Gordo was unimpressed.

"So Ryan used a cheat sheet," Gordo said with a shrug. "It's not like it was a school test. Remember, the questions were provided in advance. And nobody said these guys *couldn't* use a cheat sheet."

"Fine," said Lizzie. "But the other guys were obviously answering from memory."

"Your point?" asked Gordo.

"If Ryan used a cheat sheet on the Q&A, maybe he's being a cheat in other ways, too."

"No proof," said Gordo, shaking his head.

Was slimy Ryan the person who'd switched Ethan's questions? Lizzie wondered. Maybe with a little help from the equally snakelike Kate Sanders?

Hottie or Not-tie, Ryan Rondale was now in *first* place on Lizzie's suspect list!

8

"Mom, please pass the salt," Lizzie asked for the second time at dinner that night. "Hello? Salt? . . . MOM?"

Mrs. McGuire looked startled. "Oh, sorry, honey," she said. She quickly handed the shaker to Lizzie. "I guess I'm having a bit of trouble hearing. Your brother and Lanny have been practicing their little singing and dancing act all afternoon."

Matt dropped his fork indignantly. He was still wearing his fringed banana costume. "*Excuse* me, Mom. You're referring to an exclusive private rehearsal of The L&M Experience. The next international pop hit sensation and boy-band extreme. Just wait and see. By Saturday, Lanny and I will be—"

—the same Loser & Moron sensation I'm forced to experience every day of my life!

Lizzie stood up from the table. "May I please be excused?" she said. "Miranda and her dad will be here any minute."

"Sure, honey," Mrs. McGuire said. "You have a good time at tonight's event."

Outside, a horn honked. "That's my ride," Lizzie said. She grabbed her jean jacket and purse from the counter. "See you later!"

Matt reached for the last piece of fried chicken. "Bet on it, sister dearest," he muttered.

As the lights began to go down in the auditorium, Lizzie hurried to join Gordo. He was standing at the side of the stage, ready to begin filming this evening's Rate-A-Date event.

"This is going to be the best comedy material yet," he said. "Call it director's intuition."

Lizzie frowned. "Wait a sec. Where's Ethan?"

So far, all the contestants had taken their places in tall chairs behind the curtain. Except Ethan.

Just then, Ryan Rondale glanced at Ethan's empty chair and smiled. "Looks like Craft's a no-show," he said to Grant Castle.

"We'd better tell Mr. Wiley," Grant said. "Maybe he can stall for a while."

"Nope," Ryan said. "*Cable Entertainment* channel is broadcasting this event *live*."

The U-Can Tan theme music began to play as the curtain rose. *Oh no!* Lizzie thought. They're starting!

"Helloooo, *Fave* magazine fans!" Ty Wiley greeted the audience. "And welcome to this evening's Mr. Teen Hottie event, Rate-A-Date. Our handsome hotties will answer questions from our lovely studio bachelorettes on that all-important subject: dating!"

A spotlight swept the stage, moving from the contestants to the bachelorettes. Among the group were Miranda, Kate, and Madison.

Ty took his place at the podium. He didn't seem to notice that Ethan's chair was empty. "Bachelorette Number One," he said, "will you read our first question to the Hottie of your choice?"

There was a drum roll as Kate stepped forward, pushing Miranda and Madison out of the way. "*I'm* Bachelorette Number One," she said. "Of course."

"I've got to find Ethan," Lizzie whispered to Gordo. "Something's wrong!"

"I'll come with you," Gordo offered.

"No," Lizzie told him. "You stay here. Don't take your camera off that stage."

"Question number one is for Ryan," Kate said, in a fake-sugary voice. She paused, waiting for the audience to cheer. There was mild applause.

Kate looked down at the card one of the producers had given her before the event began. She looked at Ryan meaningfully, then read, "What qualities do you look for in a date?"

Personally, i like my chicks mean, fake, and snobby. And that's why you're my kind of girl, Kate.

Lizzie rolled her eyes. There was no time to watch Rate-a-Date now. Ethan was still missing.

She ran down the side steps from the stage and out the nearest door.

"Ethan, where are you?" Lizzie muttered

frantically. She stood in the middle of the dimly lit hall, blinking. It was hard to see anything too well after the glare of the stage's spotlight.

After her eyes focused, she spotted a crumpled piece of colorful paper lying outside the guys' dressing room. *Aha!* Lizzie thought. *A clue!* It was a wrapper from a Galaxy Burst candy—Ethan's fave.

She rushed down the hall to pick up the wrapper.

Just then, she heard a loud crash from behind the dressing room door. Then came the muffled sound of a familiar voice—

Ethan's voice, Lizzie realized.

She tried the dressing room door, but it was locked. Ethan was trapped!

"Ethan?" Lizzie called, rattling the doorknob again. "Can you hear me?"

No answer.

Lizzie pounded on the door. "Ethan, it's Lizzie! Are you okay?"

This is the part where the beautiful damsel busts open the door of the dungeon and rescues the helpless hottie dude in distress.

Just then, Lizzie heard the click-click-click of high-heeled rocker-chick boots hurrying down the hall. "What's going on here?" Amanda demanded.

Okay, correction. This is the part where the beautiful damsel fights off the fire-breathing, cell phone-wielding, leather-clad dragon and *then* rescues the dude in distress.

"Ethan's locked in the dressing room," Lizzie told Amanda. "And I just heard some kind of crash."

"Let me handle this," Amanda said. She pulled out a credit card and wedged it between the door and the doorjamb. But the door stayed locked.

"Excuse me, ladies," called a little boy's voice, "but this breaking-in business should be left to a pro."

Lizzie frowned when she saw Matt walking down the hall, still wearing his yellow Elvis jumpsuit. Lanny was right behind him.

Matt stopped in front of them, spun around on one sneaker, and said, "Please, allow me." From behind his ear, he pulled a bobby pin.

"Hey!" Lizzie said. "That's mine!"

Grinning, Matt unbent the bobby pin and jiggled it in the lock.

Suddenly, the door clicked open. Both Matt and Lanny spun around and took a bow.

"Impressive," Amanda admitted.

"Let's just say I have a fair amount of experience dealing with locked doors," Matt said. He threw Lizzie a sideways look.

So that's how the sneaky little twerp gets into my room to read my private journal. *Another* mystery solved!

Lizzie rushed into the dressing room, followed by Amanda and the boys.

Ethan stood near the window. An overturned chair lay on the floor beside him.

"Ethan, are you okay? What happened?" Lizzie asked worriedly.

Ethan ran a hand through his hair. "I dunno. Someone locked me in here by accident. I was trying to get out, but this chair kinda got in the way."

That explains the crashing noise. But the locking-in was no accident. The only question is *who* did the locking.

"I'm glad you're okay, Ethan," said Lizzie. "But right now you've got to get on stage."

"No he doesn't!" said Amanda.

Lizzie's eyes narrowed. Why didn't Ethan's own contest coach want him at his next event?

"Can't you see he has a bump on his head?" Amanda told Lizzie. She rushed up to Ethan. "Maybe you should lie down. I'll talk to Ty and straighten out your missing the Rate-A-Date event tonight."

"I'm fine, dude. Really," Ethan said. "Yo, Lizzie, wanna head to the stage with me?"

"Sure, Ethan," Lizzie said. Normally, she'd stay

to look around the room for clues, but the most important thing now was getting Ethan on stage.

Sometimes, in the grueling world of detective work, you have to set your priorities. And if that means putting your crush ahead of a case, well . . . that's just the way the magnifying glass breaks!

"Ethan babe, wait—" Amanda began to protest.

"No worries, Ms. Littlefield," Matt broke in, hooking an arm around Amanda's elbow. "I've had my share of . . . shall we say, bumps on the head, and it's never affected my ability to be oh-so clever—"

Lizzie raised an eyebrow. Maybe it wasn't so bad that Matt showed up. He could keep Amanda busy while she got Ethan out of here.

"Come on, Ethan," she whispered.

Suddenly, Madison came running up to them.

"There you are, Ethan," she said breathlessly, skidding to a stop. "They've gone to a commercial and told me to find you. You've got to be on stage in two minutes or you'll be disqualified!"

Lizzie, Madison, and Ethan ran for it. Madison and Ethan headed out onto the stage, and Lizzie returned to her backstage post beside Director Gordo.

"So, where was Boy Hottie?" he asked. "Fixing his hair?"

"Someone locked Ethan in his dressing room," Lizzie told him. "And I'm going to find out who."

After i watch the rest of Rate-a-Date. . . . Ethan's safety comes first.

Ty Wiley looked relieved as Ethan slid into his

seat. Two seconds later, the curtain rose again. The girls in the crowd went wild when they spotted Ethan. Ryan Rondale did *not* look happy.

"Hello and welcome back to our show!" Ty Wiley boomed. "We have time for just one more question. For Hottie Number Five, Ethan Craft!"

All the girls cheered. Then Madison stepped forward and read her card. "Ethan, where would you take me . . . I mean, *your date* . . . to impress her?"

Ethan scratched his head and said, "Uh . . . to the beach to catch some waves?"

"Yes indeed!" Ty Wiley broke in. "That's the best place to lather on more U-Can Tan! It works both in and out of the sun, so *you-can-tan* even at night! Ladies and gentlemen, Hottie Number Five has just earned five Perfect Date points— enough to stay in our contest!"

Phew! Lizzie thought when the curtain finally closed. That was a close one. Grant ended up winning the Rate-a-Date event, but at least Ethan hadn't been disqualified.

9

"Now we're late," Lizzie said to Gordo as they arrived at the convention center the next morning. "I can't believe my parents made me take *them*."

She glanced over her shoulder and shuddered. Today Matt and Lanny were wearing bright blue jumpsuits with "L" and "M" glued on their chests in rhinestones.

"You won't even know we're here," Matt said. Lanny nodded in agreement. "But Amanda Littlefield will," insisted Matt. "She's the pro we're set to impress—"

"Just stay out of my way, you Smurf-colored twerp," Lizzie told him.

i've already got my hands full protecting Ethan, which i'm sure he'll appreciate . . . er, sooner or later.

"You know, this Dancing Dudes event may put things over the top for my comedy portfolio," Gordo said. "Ethan is one seriously pitiful dancer."

Lizzie frowned. "His style is just a little . . . different," she told Gordo, "that's all. I'm sure the contest choreographer will help him in this practice session."

"They only have *one hour*," Gordo noted.

Lizzie, Gordo, and the boys walked into the auditorium just as the five hottie contestants were climbing onto the stage.

The choreographer, a bearded man wearing a silk shirt and velvet jeans, stood at the base of the stage with a big boom box. "Okay, boys," he said. "You've heard the song a few times at this point, so you should have the beat in your head. Now, I want to see your basic moves—and I'll do my best to improve them. Let's begin."

Lizzie and Gordo found Miranda sitting a few rows back from the stage in the big, empty auditorium. She had gotten to the rehearsal early to chat with Grant. And she also promised Lizzie she'd keep an eye out for "any suspicious activity."

"Don't worry," Miranda said when Lizzie and Gordo sat down. "You didn't miss anything. And before you ask, *no*, I did *not* notice any suspicious activity. The best thing about my coming early was Grant. He and I had a really great talk."

"Great," Lizzie said. "Thanks." But secretly she suspected that the only reason Miranda "didn't notice any suspicious activity" was because she'd been totally distracted by Grant.

As far as Lizzie was concerned, Grant was still a viable suspect. Lizzie glanced around the seats. Kate was busy signing Ryan's name on photos. Madison was sitting in the front row, watching Ethan with rapt attention. And Amanda was writing furiously on her Palm Pilot. Lizzie saw Matt and Lanny sit down right behind Amanda. Matt tried to read the woman's notes over her shoulder. She turned around to glare at him.

When "Summer Don't Go" by a new group called Surf boomed from the speakers, Amanda's attention snapped to the front. She watched the five hottie contestants dance around for ten seconds, then she jumped to her feet. "Stop!" she called.

Everyone, including the choreographer, turned to stare at Amanda.

"What is she doing?" Lizzie whispered. Gordo and Miranda shrugged.

"Ryan's a problem," Amanda complained. "His moves are pushing Ethan all over the stage, and I won't have it. Ethan, I want you on that black X I marked down in front. And you, the redhead in the black T-shirt, you're too tall to dance next to Ethan. You make him look short."

The choreographer frowned. "Lady, this is *my* show. Would you please sit down?"

"Ethan, you heard me!" called Amanda.

Ethan shrugged and moved to the spot Amanda had designated for him.

"Okay, boys," said the choreographer, "some of you look a little stiff. Now, I want you to relax. *Feel* the music. *Be* the music." The music started up again.

Ten seconds later, Amanda called out, "Cut! Ryan's trying to upstage Ethan again!"

"Whoa," Matt said to Lanny. "She's as tough as Melina. . . . I'm *impressed.*"

Now the choreographer looked even more annoyed. He flipped off the music. "Look, I'm in charge here," he told Amanda. "And I don't need any help, thank you very much."

Amanda put her hand on her hip. "Mr. Craft is my client," she said. "And I can't allow you to allow him to look like a fool."

"I don't think it's the choreographer's fault," Gordo muttered to Lizzie. "Check out the action over there."

Lizzie turned to see Ethan near the front of the stage. He didn't seem to notice that the music had stopped. Caught up in his own creative voguing, he was flailing his arm in strange, jerky motions.

"*Feel* the music," he was murmuring, eyes closed. "*Be* the music. . . ."

Suddenly, he slipped on an orange puddle of U-Can Tan. It had spilled from one of the zillions of bottles displayed along the stage front. They were part of the sponsor's stage decorations for that evening's final events.

Instantly, Ethan hit the floor and grimaced in pain.

"Oh, no!" Lizzie cried. "He's hurt!" She rushed

toward the stage—but not before she saw Ryan laughing. *Creep*, she thought angrily.

By the time Lizzie reached Ethan, Amanda and Madison were already at his side.

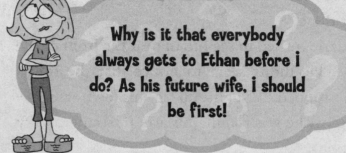

Why is it that everybody always gets to Ethan before i do? As his future wife, i should be first!

"Poor baby," Madison crooned. "Do you want me to get you some ice?"

"Are you really injured?" Amanda asked anxiously standing over Ethan. She bent down and touched his ankle gingerly with her right hand.

Miranda and Gordo walked up to Lizzie. "Will he be okay?" Miranda whispered.

"I hope so," Lizzie said. Amanda was standing up again. She seemed so upset that she didn't even seem to care that a large drop of U-Can Tan had turned her multi-braceleted left hand bright orange.

"I feel like this is all my fault—" said Lizzie.

"Lizzie, it was an *accident*," Gordo said. "There was nothing you could do. The guy just tripped over his own feet, that's all."

"No," Lizzie said, frowning. "He tripped on a puddle of U-Can Tan. Maybe someone spilled it there on purpose."

"You'll have to stay off your feet, Ethan," Amanda was saying now. "But don't worry, babe. You'll have other chances."

Other chances? Lizzie thought. The Mr. Teen Hottie contest came only once a year! Plus, if Ethan dropped out, that jerk Ryan Rondale might win again—which the sneaky creep didn't deserve, Lizzie noted to herself. Right now he was taking a long swig from his water bottle, acting as if nothing had happened.

"I'm going to do some investigating," Lizzie told her friends through gritted teeth.

"We'll come with you," Miranda said.

Lizzie walked over and picked up the U-Can Tan bottle that had spilled. There was a big hole punched in the bottom.

"Look at this!" she told her friends. "Someone *made* the bottle leak on purpose."

Quickly, Lizzie checked out the other bottles lined along the stage. None of them had holes. "And look at *this*," she said. "All the *other* bottles are *empty*."

"Wow," Miranda said. "You mean those bottles are fake?"

Lizzie nodded. "They're obviously just here for decoration," she said. "But somebody put a *real* bottle near that X Amanda had marked for Ethan—and made sure it leaked its contents so there would be a puddle for Ethan to slip on. Sabotage set up to look like an accident. Just like that hitch pin at the parade."

"Yeah, that's possible," Gordo said slowly. "But still—"

"Hey, wait a sec," Lizzie said, frowning. She looked down again at the puddle on the floor. It was bright orange!

She checked the label again. According to the directions, U-Can Tan was clear when it came out of the bottle—invisible on the skin. It didn't change color, or "tan," until at least thirty minutes after being exposed to the air.

"So that means the bottle had to be spilled over half an hour ago," Lizzie murmured. "Before I got here for sure." She turned to Miranda. "Who went up on the stage this morning? You were here before me."

Miranda bit her lip. "There was a lot of activity, so I'm not sure exactly . . ."

"Because you were talking to Grant, right?" Lizzie guessed.

"Sorry, Lizzie," said Miranda.

"It's okay," said Lizzie. She looked around the room for possible suspects. Amanda was frantically trying to place a call on her cell phone.

Grant was trying to help Ethan stand up on his bad ankle. Madison had run off for an ice pack.

But Ryan Rondale was leaning against the official Mr. Teen Hottie throne at the other side of the stage, chuckling as he watched Ethan hobble along on Grant's shoulder.

Ryan's not just a jerk . . . he's a *very suspicious* jerk.

But just as Lizzie was about to march over and question Ryan, she heard Amanda click her cell phone shut.

"Sorry, Ethan babe," Amanda said. "I just talked to Ty Wiley and gave him the news. You're going to have to drop out of the Mr. Teen Hottie contest."

10

"Drop out of the contest?" Ethan frowned at his manager. "No way, dude. I told you, I'm going to Hawaii."

Amanda tucked her phone in a pocket of her leather jacket. "Sorry, sugar. Doesn't look like you have a choice. You're injured."

The choreographer spoke up. "I hate to say it, but she's right. Sprains can sideline dancers for weeks."

"Oh, not that long," Amanda said, with a wave. "A couple of days, and he'll be good as new."

Lizzie and Miranda looked at each other. "Ethan definitely won't be able to perform in the Dancing Dudes number," Miranda whispered. "It starts in less than an hour!"

"Yep, looks like Ethan's big shot at fame and fortune is history," Gordo said, filming away on his video camera. "Hey, maybe I can sell this as a tearjerker documentary: *A Hottie's Dream Shattered.*"

"Not so fast," called a boy's voice. "Make way, please. I have a merit badge in first aid."

Lizzie cringed. Matt again!

Her little brother was pushing through the crowd, carrying a first-aid kit and a roll of bandages. Madison followed with a zillion bags of ice.

"Does he really know what he's doing?" Miranda asked as Matt expertly began to wrap Ethan's ankle.

"Well," Lizzie said, "Matt *did* administer proper first aid to my dad once—after the little poisonous pest caused my father's injuries in the first place. So, *yes*, Matt knows what he's doing."

And so do i, which means whoever set Ethan up to get hurt had better watch out—because even if my crush-boy does drop out of the contest, i am going to solve this case!

An hour later, Lizzie was standing in front of an outdoor stage in Hillridge Park. A huge lunchtime crowd had gathered to watch the Dancing Dudes event of the Mr. Teen Hottie pageant.

Thanks to ice packs and lots of attention from paramedic Matt, Ethan had managed to recover enough to enter the dance number.

"Your little brother is a hero!" Madison gushed to Lizzie. "Ethan's ankle is as good as new."

"Sort of," Lizzie said. "I can't believe he's actually up there dancing."

"Ethan has his own unique style, don't you think?" Madison said.

"Unique. You could say that," Miranda muttered. Then she gestured for Lizzie to look behind them. "Looks like Amanda over there isn't too happy."

Lizzie turned around. Ethan's coach was nervously nibbling her magenta fingernails as Ethan slid and jerked his way through the song "Summer Don't Go." Luckily, the crowd loved the whole number. Girls screamed and cheered as their favorite contestants took turns dancing at the front of the stage.

Amanda actually covered her eyes as Ethan

stepped forward and struck a pose. "Oh no!" the woman said when she finally moved one hand to peek. "Ethan, sugar, what are you *doing*?"

Lizzie looked back at the stage. Ethan had gotten so caught up in his own thing that he lost the beat and ran into Ryan. Then he completely blocked the other two guys from stepping forward, and hit Grant in the face by mistake.

The crowd roared with laughter as the hotties bumped into each other. Ryan looked furious.

"Hilarious," Gordo said from behind his camera. "You can't script this kind of stuff."

Suddenly, there was a rustling from the fake Hawaiian flowers at the back of the outdoor stage. Matt and Lanny, wearing their blue jump-suits, burst through the backdrop.

Now it was Lizzie's turn to shut her eyes. "Tell me this isn't happening," she said to Miranda.

"You know," Miranda said as Matt and Lanny began to move through their own routine, "they're not so bad."

Miranda was right. Even Lizzie had to admit that the L&M Experience was a welcome distraction. The crowd loved it. Even Amanda was tapping a spike-heeled boot.

When the Dancing Dudes event mercifully ended, Ethan had fallen behind in points. But there seemed to be no clear winner—except Gordo. "I've got to get more film," he said eagerly.

Ty Wiley's voice boomed through the speakers. "Let's hear it for our Dancing Dudes!"

Lizzie moved forward to catch up with Ethan, but a crowd of girls swarmed him—and all the other contestants.

When she saw Ryan Rondale, the reigning Mr. Teen Hottie, break free and quickly move toward the Contestants Only area, she followed.

As she got closer, she heard Ryan talking in a low voice to the tall redheaded contestant. "Craft made us all look bad. He should have stayed down—and out," Ryan muttered. "At tonight's Formal Evening finals, I'm *personally* taking the guy out for good. He won't stand a chance."

Lizzie shrank back against a fence as Ryan disappeared into the contestants' area.

That's a definite threat. I've got to warn Ethan!

Lizzie waited for Ethan to walk over. There were more girls hanging on to him now than ever. "Gotta go, dudettes," he told them apologetically.

"Ethan, wait!" Lizzie called before he stepped into the restricted area. "I've got to talk to you."

Ethan threw a U-Can Tan towel over his shoulder. "Sure, Lizzie," he said, coming over. "What's up?"

Lizzie told him her suspicions about the U-Can Tan puddle being a setup *and* Ryan being her prime suspect—especially after what she'd just overheard.

"Ethan, you have to trust me on this," she told him urgently. "You have to keep your eyes open. You don't know what Ryan might do. Things could get really dangerous!"

"Lizzie, Lizzie, Lizzie," Ethan said. "You worry too much, you know? . . . But I *am* beginning to think that maybe you've got a point here."

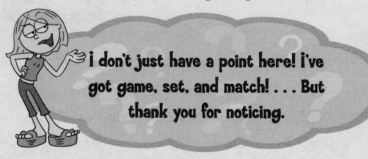

i don't just have a point here! i've got game, set, and match! . . . But thank you for noticing.

Ethan leaned forward. "So, Lizzie," he said, "do you think you could do me a favor?"

"Sure, Ethan," Lizzie said eagerly. "Name it."

"Well, I still need to choose a girl to escort on stage tonight," he said. "You know, for that Formal Evening deal?"

Lizzie's heart pounded. "Oh. I forgot all about that," she lied. "Have you asked anyone yet?"

"It's kinda hard to decide," Ethan said with a sigh. "A lot of girls have asked *me*."

"Oh," Lizzie said. "Right."

"Anyway, Lizzie, I'm thinking, maybe I should ask you," Ethan went on. "Since we're just friends and all."

Just friends?
How can you say that about
your future wife?

Lizzie cleared her throat. "Sure, Ethan, no problem. That'd be great."

Now all I need is a dress, glass slippers, and a really big pumpkin. Oh, and Fairy Godmother? While you're at it, some bling-bling would be much appreciated.

11

"Lizzie, I need your hair goop!" Matt called through the bedroom door.

Lizzie sighed and went over to open the door a tiny crack. "Here," she said, thrusting out the tube of gel. "But give it back fast. I need it."

Matt blocked Lizzie from closing the door. "So what do you think of this look?" he asked. "Keep in mind that Lanny and I are dressing to impress Amanda Littlefield. She's just the right talent scout to recognize our brilliance—and she's letting us audition for her tonight."

Lizzie just stared at her little brother, speechless. Miranda peered over her shoulder. "Very, uh . . . colorful," she said.

Matt had blown dry his hair so it stood up in every direction. He wore a purple jacket and striped pants. His sneakers were red and he had added a yellow scarf around his neck.

"Clown City," Lizzie said. "Now, go away."

"Lizzie, be nice to your brother," Mrs. McGuire said, coming by with a laundry basket. "This is his big night, you know."

"It's *my* big night, too," Lizzie protested.

Hello? This is the first date of the rest of my life with Ethan Craft! Um, hello? HELLO???

"You look very nice, dear," Ms. McGuire said. Lizzie stared into the mirror at her long pink dress. The layers of glittery chiffon over the silky skirt made her feel like some really cool princess. "Do you think maybe this is overkill?" she asked her friend.

"Nope," Miranda said. "You look great."

"So do you," said Lizzie.

Miranda was wearing a long red-and-black plaid skirt with a black velvet top that laced up the back. It was the perfect outfit to go with Miranda's dark hair and funky style.

"Well, I hope Grant agrees," Miranda said. "I'm so excited that he asked me to be his escort tonight."

Lizzie was happy for her friend. But it was still possible that Grant was trying to make Ethan drop out of the contest. Can Mr. Nice Guy really be trusted? she wondered.

"I know you still think Grant is a suspect," Miranda said as she helped Lizzie with the curling iron. "But don't worry, I'll keep an eye on him for you. Better yet, I'll keep *both* eyes on him!"

She twisted another lock of Lizzie's long blond hair around the curling iron. "Ouch!" she cried. "I burned my thumb!"

"I'll get you some ice," Lizzie said. "Just call me Madison."

Miranda grinned as she stuck her finger in her mouth. "No, I'm okay. I'm just not very talented with this thing, I guess."

"Ohmigosh!" Lizzie gasped. "We forgot something really important!"

"What?" Miranda asked, frowning.

"There's a *talent* event right before the Formal Evening deal," Lizzie said. "Ethan needs a *talent*!"

"Does Ethan *have* any talents?" Miranda asked.

"Not sure," Lizzie admitted. "There's only one thing to do." She picked up the phone beside her bed. "Let's call Gordo!"

"Relax," Gordo said, when Lizzie told him the problem. "I've already got it covered."

"You do?" Lizzie asked.

"Yeah, I kind of anticipated this," Gordo said.

"But I've got to go help Ethan set up, okay? I'll see you later."

"Thanks, Gordo," Lizzie told him. "You're the best."

In the car on the way to the convention center, Lizzie nervously twisted the strap of her sparkly pink bag. She still wasn't *absolutely* sure Ryan was the one who'd been sabotaging Ethan—even though he seemed the most likely one.

She kept going over the events in her head: the warning on the sunblock, the float's loose hitch pin at the parade, the switched Q&A questions, the locked dressing room door, the spilled tanning lotion. . . .

Lizzie reached into her bag and took out a small notepad. She went over the case again, trying to figure out who had been where, and when. The problem was, almost all of her suspects had always been around whenever something happened to Ethan.

If Ethan could just get through the evening, he might be the next Mr. Teen Hottie. But if something went wrong again . . .

Beside her, Miranda held up both her arms. "I am so pale," she moaned. "I think I need a good blast of U-Can Tan. I look like a ghost."

Matt twisted around in his seat. "If you used U-Can Tan, you'd look like a pumpkin," he said.

"That's right, Miranda," Lizzie teased. "You could have that all-natural neon-orange tan in just thirty minutes or your—"

Suddenly, Lizzie stopped and stared at her friend. "Ohmigosh, that's it!" she cried. "I've solved the mystery!"

CHAPTER

12

"Huh?" Miranda said. "You mean you know who's been sabotaging Ethan?"

"I think so," Lizzie said. She leaned forward in her seat. "Dad, can you drive faster? The talent competition starts in five minutes. We'll be late!"

"Sorry, honey, there's a lot of traffic around the convention center," Mr. McGuire said.

"Lizzie, *tell* me! Who's trying to stop Ethan from becoming Mr. Teen Hottie?" Miranda demanded. "I'm dying from the suspense here."

But Lizzie was concentrating on the dashboard clock. "Look, it's seven o'clock!" she cried. "We're never going to make it! I have to reach Ethan before it's too late!"

Mr. McGuire swung the car up to the front of the convention center. Lizzie, Miranda, and the boys jumped out and pushed through a disappointed crowd of ticketless Mr. Teen Hottie fans.

The talent competition was already in progress. Ryan Rondale was on stage, singing a rather lame version of a popular song. But the girls in the crowd loved it anyway. They were squealing and swooning.

Yuck! thought Lizzie.

"Let's get backstage," she told Miranda.

As they hurried down the side aisle of the darkened auditorium, Ryan finished his number. Grant took the stage next, with his dog, Rudi.

"The next hottie contestant in our talent competition is Grant Castle," Ty Wiley announced. "Grant will be performing a dog-training exhibition with his black Lab, Rudi."

"Oooh, can we stop and watch?" Miranda asked Lizzie. "I really want to see Grant."

Lizzie looked down at the program she'd been handed at the door. Ethan was after Grant. "Well, okay." She sighed.

Grant and Rudi's dog tricks were a big hit with the crowd. "Isn't Grant the best?" Miranda said, her eyes shining.

"What about Ethan?" Lizzie asked, as Ethan walked on stage.

"Well, they're both great, I guess," Miranda said. "May the hottest hottie win!"

"And our last but not least contestant is Ethan Craft," Ty Wiley announced. "Now here's a guy who really has fun in the U-Can sun—Ethan's talent is surfing, dudes!"

Ethan pretended to hang-ten on the edge of the stage. He waved to his cheering fans. Then a movie screen began to move down from the ceiling behind him.

"Ethan, get out of the way!" Lizzie heard

Gordo call to him from the wings.

Ethan moved and the lights dimmed in the auditorium. The words "*Surfer Dude*: A Film by David Gordon" appeared on the screen.

"How cool is that?" Miranda said. "Gordo's showing that video he made of Ethan surfing last summer."

"Gordo always comes through," Lizzie said. "Even for Ethan. He's the best!"

When the video ended, Ty announced the results of the talent event. Grant was first, Ethan was second—and Ryan was third.

Ryan's really going to be mad now, thought Lizzie. And, sure enough, Ryan stormed off the stage as soon as the curtains began to close.

"We've got to get backstage," Lizzie told Miranda. "The Formal Evening event is next— and I have some business to take care of first."

As soon as they showed their Escort IDs and stepped through the stage door, Lizzie spotted Ryan sitting in the corner. He was sulking, as usual.

Amanda Littlefield was standing over him, talking very fast. "Ryan, sweetie, forget about this stupid contest," Lizzie heard her say. "Go for the big bucks! So what if your singing's a little weak? You can lip synch! The important thing is, you can *dance*! I can get you gigs, babe. And—"

With Miranda on her heels, Lizzie marched over to Ethan's pushy manager. "Okay, Amanda," said Lizzie. "You're busted. Why have you been sabotaging Ethan?"

"Her!" Miranda blurted out, stunned. "*Amanda's* the guilty party?"

Amanda whirled angrily. "Get lost," she told Lizzie sharply. "We're talking business here."

Lizzie stood her ground. "You were around Ethan every time something went wrong. And—"

"You've got the wrong person, Blondie," Amanda said. "And time is money, so scram."

"No. I *know* you're the one who sabotaged Ethan," Lizzie insisted. "The proof is right there in your hand."

"Huh?" Amanda said. She looked down at the cell phone in her right hand.

"Your *left* hand," Lizzie told her. "It's got a huge orange spot on it." She turned and grinned back at Miranda. "*Pumpkin* orange."

"Am I missing something here?" Amanda snapped.

"I'll fill you in," Lizzie said. "When Ethan got hurt at the Dancing Dudes rehearsal, your left hand had that same orange spot. You obviously got it when you spilled the U-Can Tan for Ethan to slip on."

"You're crazy," Amanda said. "It got on me when I went to help him."

"I watched you. You touched his ankle with your *right* hand only," Lizzie said. "And since U-Can Tan is invisible when it first contacts the skin, you obviously didn't realize it would show up on your left hand. It turns orange thirty minutes *after* contact."

"Whoa, *impressive*," said Miranda.

Amanda began to sputter.

"And there's more," said Lizzie. "At the reception dinner, you left the dance floor to make a *very* long call—that's when you obviously wrote that warning note on the bottle of sunblock. You were the one who loosened the hitch pin at the parade. You switched the Q&A questions, before giving the packet to Madison to give to Ethan. And you were also the one who locked Ethan in the guys' dressing room, too, which is why you were on the scene so quickly. What I couldn't figure out was *why*. Why did you do it?"

"*Why?* No reason!" Amanda said frantically. "I'm Ethan's coach. Why would I want to sabotage him? I don't have a motive, Blondie. So you must have the wrong person."

"Oh, no, I don't," Lizzie said. "Because I've just figured that out, too. What's the reason my little brother is trying so hard to impress you? Because you're a talent scout. And the morning of the parade, I heard you talking on your cell phone, behind a garment rack. You said you badly needed a big break because of a career slump and you finally had an 'interesting new prospect.' Ethan is that prospect—you want him to be your big new 'discovery.' But if Ethan wins Mr. Teen Hottie tonight, he'll be tied up for a whole year promoting U-Can Tan. That's according to his contract—the very contract you said that you were upset he'd signed on the first night of the pageant."

So HA! Score one for Blondie!

Amanda frowned. "Fine. Okay. So what."

"You admit it then?" asked Lizzie, almost a little surprised. "You were trying to blow Ethan's chances of winning."

"Look, try to understand," said Amanda. "When

I saw Ethan's karaoke number at the reception dinner that first night—and the reactions from all the girls—I thought I'd discovered my new star. I wasn't going to risk his being tied down with a year of Mr. Teen Hottie responsibilities."

Miranda stepped up. "But how could you sabotage your own cousin's stepson like that?"

Amanda shrugged. "It was for his own good. Ethan had signed all those forms and contracts already, so he couldn't drop out for no reason. And the poor kid actually wanted to win the contest, so I didn't think I could change his mind. It wasn't personal or anything. It was just business."

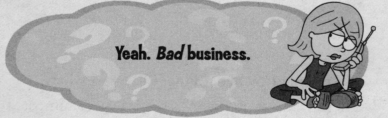

Yeah. *Bad* business.

"The thing is," said Amanda, "I changed my mind about Ethan's potential at the Dancing Dudes event."

"What?" cried Lizzie.

"I mean, sure, Ethan can wow a crowd with a karaoke rap—but he's a *rotten* dancer. It would take way too much work to give him some decent moves. And time is money."

"That's terrible," Lizzie said.

"It's the biz, Blondie," said Amanda. She jerked her head toward Ryan, who gave Lizzie a pearly smile. "Now Ryan here can dance—*and* sing. Sort of. And I'm putting my money on him to lose tonight's contest."

Ryan's big smile disappeared.

Just then, Ty Wiley called all the contestants and their escorts to the stage for the Formal Evening event.

i'll deal with Amanda later. Right now it's time for me to stand beside the hottie of my dreams!

"Lizzie, Lizzie, Lizzie," Ethan said as he took Lizzie's arm. "You look really pretty, dude."

"Thanks," Lizzie said, smiling up at Ethan. He looked more gorgeous than ever in a Hawaiian blue tux with a yellow bow tie.

Most guys could never pull off that look, Lizzie thought. But on Ethan the outfit looked great.

Quickly, she filled him in about Amanda's dirty tricks. Ethan eyes widened. "Whoa," he said, "that is *so* not cool."

"Should we go to Ty Wiley?" asked Lizzie.

"Explain everything. Maybe the judges can award you extra points because of the sabotage."

"Nah," said Ethan, shaking his head. "Maybe if it was another contestant doing the dirty tricks. But it was my own coach!"

"That's true," said Lizzie. "But it's still a raw deal for you."

"Yeah," said Ethan. "But, dude, it's not over yet. Let's just be cool and take our chances."

Seconds later, they were entering the spotlight. As each couple stepped onto the stage, the crowd went wild.

"I'm so glad I wore this tiara," Kate whispered to Lizzie on stage. "It'll match Ryan's *crown* perfectly. Don't you think?"

Lizzie just rolled her eyes. Even Kate can't ruin this night, she told herself. I'm standing here with Ethan!

"It's time to ask our hotties the big final question," Ty Wiley announced. "Grant, you'll go first."

Grant stepped to the front of the stage.

"Just answer 'world peace'!" Miranda called to her escort in loud whisper.

"All right, Grant Castle," Ty said. "Who is your best buddy and why?"

"I guess that would be Rudi," Grant said. "She's the best, most loyal friend a guy could have. She's always there for me."

The audience applauded loudly. "Oh, isn't that cuuuute?" Lizzie overheard a girl say. "He loves his doggy!"

"Next is Ethan Craft," Ty said. "Ethan, who is your best buddy and why?"

Ethan scratched his head. "Well, that's a tough one. But I'd have to say Lizzie McGuire. She always watches my back, you know?"

Everyone clapped again.

Okay, so "best buddy" isn't very romantic, but I have to admit— it's pretty awesome he said it.

After all the contestants had answered the final question and the points were tallied up, the time came to announce the winner.

"All right, we have the envelope," Ty Wiley said, ripping it open. Our first runner-up and the winner of our Mr. Teen Nice Guy crown is . . . Ethan Craft!"

The crowd cheered and whistled. Lizzie watched Ethan go up to get his crown, a cool new surfboard—and a certificate for a lifetime supply of U-Can Tan. All in all, he looked pretty happy.

"And the winner of *Fave* Magazine's Mr. Teen Hottie contest is: Grant Castle!"

Miranda screamed and jumped up and down as Grant went up to receive his Mr. Hottie crown, his scholarship, his trip to Hawaii—and more U-Can Tan. Rudi bounded onto the stage and ran around in circles.

Finally, the curtain closed and Ryan Rondale got his consolation prize—the undivided attention of Amanda Littlefield.

"Oh, too bad," Lizzie and Miranda said to Kate after they left the stage, their arms full or roses. Then they both looked at each other and added, "Not!"

That's when Lizzie saw Matt and Lanny walk past in a hurry. Melina was with them, looking very miffed.

"No way," she heard Melina say. "The L&M Experience does *not* do backup. Tell that Amanda person it's top billing or nothing!"

When Gordo finally caught up with Lizzie and Miranda, he noticed Lizzie was wearing Ethan's Mr. Nice Guy crown on her head.

"He gave it to me before all his groupies surrounded him," Lizzie explained.

Then she told Gordo the whole story of Amanda's sabotaging Ethan.

"You know," said Miranda, "maybe Ethan should talk to Amanda anyway. Try to change her mind about Ryan—and get her to take him on as a client."

"Miranda! Are you crazy!" said Gordo.

"Hey, after that woman messed up his chances of winning Mr. Teen Hottie, don't you think she owes him?" said Miranda.

"No way," said Gordo. "Anyone who tries to manipulate you instead of being straight with you is one dangerous sneak. The last thing you want to do is trust a person like that with your image—and your rep."

"And your future," Lizzie added. She reached up and took Ethan's Mr. Nice Guy crown from her head and placed it on Gordo's.

"What's this for?" asked Gordo.

Lizzie smiled. "Let's just say I think this should go to you," she told him. "'Cause you're not only my best friend, you're the nicest guy I know."

Case closed!

Lizzie McGuire MYSTERIES

Want to have a way cool time? Here's a clue. . . . Read the next Lizzie McGuire Mystery!

CASE OF THE DOGGONE DOGS

To raise money for an animal shelter, Lizzie starts her own dog-walking and dog-sitting business. But when cheerleaders Kate and Claire try to steal her canine clients for their pom-pom fund-raiser, Lizzie fights back by cutting her fees and collaring Miranda and Gordo to help. Then someone deliberately lets the dogs out of the McGuires' backyard and Lizzie is howling mad. Can she track down the lost dogs *and* sniff out the guilty party before *she* ends up in the doghouse?

"Just call me Snoop Dog McGuire!"